The Mystery of the Birthday Party

THREE COUSINS DETECTIVE CLUB®

The Mystery of the Birthday Party

Elspeth Campbell Murphy
Illustrated by Joe Nordstrom

BETHANY HOUSE PUBLISHERS
MINNEAPOLIS, MINNESOTA 55438

Published by Bethany House Publishers
A Ministry of Bethany Fellowship International
11400 Hampshire Avenue South
Minneapolis, Minnesota 55438
www.bethanyhouse.com

Printed in the United States of America by
Bethany Press International, Minneapolis, Minnesota 55438

Library of Congress Cataloging-in-Publication Data

Murphy, Elspeth Campbell.
    The mystery of the birthday party / by Elspeth Campbell Murphy.
        p. cm. — (Three Cousins Detective Club ; #17)
    Summary: When their neighbors appear to be throwing a birthday party
for their dog, the three cousins suspect that things are not what they seem.
    ISBN 1-55661-855-7 (pbk.)
    [1. Dogs—Fiction. 2. Birthdays—Fiction. 3. Parties—Fiction.
4. Cousins—Fiction. 5. Mystery and detective stories.] I. Title.
II. Series: Murphy, Elspeth Campbell. Three Cousins Detective Club ; 17.
PZ7.M95316Mj   1997
[Fic]—dc21   97–21121
                                                    CIP
                                                    AC

ELSPETH CAMPBELL MURPHY has been a familiar name in Christian publishing for over fifteen years, with more than seventy-five books to her credit and sales reaching five million worldwide. She is the author of the best-selling series *David and I Talk to God* and *The Kids From Apple Street Church*, as well as the 1990 Gold Medallion winner *Do You See Me, God?* A graduate of Trinity College and Moody Bible Institute, Elspeth and her husband, Mike, make their home in Chicago, where she writes full time.

Contents

"Don't make plans to hurt your neighbor. He lives nearby and trusts you."

Proverbs 3:29

1

$\mathcal{B}ANG!$

BANG!

Titus McKay and his cousins Sarah-Jane Cooper and Timothy Dawson jumped.

"Yo!" gulped Titus. *"What* was *that?"*

"It sounded like a *cannon* going off!" exclaimed Timothy.

"But it sounded so *close!*" gasped Sarah-Jane.

The cousins sat up and looked around them. The truth was, they were feeling a little groggy, and the sudden noise had really scared them.

They would never in a million years have *planned* to take a nap after lunch. But they had worked hard all morning. The day was warm. And they had been eating lunch in a tree house. So—what with the gentle rustling of the leaves—they had just sort of dozed off. Dozed, that is, until they had been jolted awake by the mysterious bang.

The three cousins had a detective club. They liked solving mysteries. And it didn't take them long to solve this one.

Dangling from a branch above them was a scrap of rubber with a string tied to one end.

A balloon.

Only a burst balloon.

The cousins laughed, feeling a little embarrassed.

Titus, who was especially good at climbing, scrambled higher up the tree to get the balloon scrap.

When he climbed down with it, the cousins gathered around to take a closer look. They could still make out the words *Happy Birthday* in little letters. (The cousins knew the words would have been big when the balloon was blown up.)

This was interesting! Quickly they looked around for a party. They saw one. Or at least the decorations for a party. It was in the yard across the alley.

There were some other letters on the balloon beside the ones that said *Happy Birthday*.

A name, maybe?

Always curious, Titus pushed the pieces together so that he could read it.

"Hmm," he said. "That's funny!"

"Funny ha-ha? Or funny weird?" asked Timothy.

"Funny weird," said Titus.

"What's funny weird?" asked Sarah-Jane.

"The name on the balloon," said Titus. "It says *Maggie*."

"What's weird about that?" asked Sarah-Jane. "I like the name Maggie. I know two different girls who are named that."

"I agree with you that it's a nice name," said Titus. "It's just that the only Maggie who lives in the house across the alley is a poodle."

2

Dog-Person

*T*itus was a true "dog-person." He knew all the dogs in the neighborhood by name and personality.

And this wasn't even his neighborhood.

Even though he had a tree house in it.

Titus lived in a big apartment building in the city. The yard where he had his tree house was also in the city. But it was in a neighborhood of old houses and big trees. This was where his granduncle Frank and grandaunt Barbara lived.

They were like Titus's grandparents on his father's side.

Titus's real grandparents on his father's side had died years and years before Titus was even born. In fact, they had died when Titus's father was still a teenager. So he had gone to live with his father's sister Barbara and her husband, Frank. They were like his second parents, and he loved them very much.

Frank and Barbara's last name was Titus. So when Titus came along, he was named after his father's aunt and uncle. He got their last name for his first name.

Frank and Barbara were absolutely crazy about Titus—which is why they built a tree house for him in their yard.

Timothy and Sarah-Jane were not related to Frank and Barbara Titus at all. (The cousins were related to one another on their mothers' side. Their mothers were sisters.)

But Timothy and Sarah-Jane knew Frank and Barbara from when Timothy and Sarah-Jane visited Titus. They called them Granduncle Frank and Grandaunt Barbara, just as Titus did. You couldn't call people Mr. and Mrs. Titus when you had a cousin named Titus. It was just too funny-sounding.

To make matters even more complicated, there were dogs involved.

A sleepy old dog named Wags.

And a peppy youngster named Gubbio.

Wags was the Tituses' dog.

And Gubbio was Titus's dog.

Now both dogs looked up at the tree house and barked.

Neither one of them cared for heights. So they weren't barking to get up in the tree house. They were barking for their dog-people to come down and play with them.

Titus shoved the little scrap of balloon into his pocket and looked over the tree house railing.

"OK, we're coming!" he said to Gubbio and Wags. "Just hold your horses."

The dogs stopped barking and looked at him in surprise. Horses? What horses? They didn't have any horses. Sometimes humans said the *strangest* things!

3

Sweet Dogs

*T*he cousins gathered up their lunch litter and put it in a basket.

Tied to the handle of the basket was one end of a long rope. The other end of the rope was tied to the tree house railing. That way, the cousins could lower the basket to the ground before they climbed down the ladder. It left their hands free for holding on.

If they wanted to bring something up to the tree house, they put it in the basket on the ground. Then they could climb up the ladder. And, as soon as they were settled, they could pull up the basket.

It was a system Titus had thought up a long time ago, and it worked like a charm. The cousins had even managed to get a pizza up to

the tree house for lunch.

The only problem was, one of them had to stand guard if Wags and Gubbio were around—at least until the basket was too high for the dogs to reach.

Gubbio always wanted people food, and he could jump pretty high.

Wags liked people food, too, but he never jumped at all if he could help it.

The cousins had the same problem coming down. One of them had to be there to grab the basket before the dogs could get it.

The family had been doing house projects all morning. The last thing anyone needed was to have shreds of a pizza box all over the yard. So Titus went down first and grabbed the basket that Timothy and Sarah-Jane lowered to him.

Gubbio looked disappointed.

"People food is not good for dogs," Titus said to Gubbio. "If I tell you 'no,' it's because I love you. We've talked about this before, remember? The vet said you can have a few little table scraps from dinner, but that's it."

If Gubbio remembered, he wasn't going to admit it. But he didn't get mad about it, either. He and Wags were two of the sweetest dogs in the world.

Maggie was a sweet dog, too. A beautiful, full-size black poodle with dark, intelligent eyes.

Thinking of Maggie reminded Titus of the scrap of birthday balloon in his pocket. And thinking of the scrap of birthday balloon reminded him of a question he had to ask his granduncle Frank.

4

A Peculiar Question

*I*t was a standing joke in Titus's family that he was always FULL of questions. And he had been known to ask some pretty unusual ones. Lately he had started making up some funny ones as a kind of running gag he had with Granduncle Frank. Frank would laugh and say, "Good one, Titus!"

The problem was—what if you had a serious question that only *sounded* funny?

Titus asked it anyway.

"Granduncle Frank, did Wags happen to get an invitation to a birthday party?"

Frank laughed. "Good one, Titus!"

"No—*seriously*!" said Titus.

"Seriously?" replied Frank in surprise. "No, Wags did not get an invitation to a birthday party. And I would have remembered that—because Wags doesn't get a lot of mail. Why in the world are you asking?"

"Because Maggie's having a birthday party," said Titus. "And it sure seems like Wags should have been invited. Gubbio, too, since he's here so much."

"Maggie—?" said his uncle. "Maggie who? You don't mean—Maggie the *poodle*?"

"The one who lives across the alley," said Sarah-Jane.

"Right," said Frank.

"Right," said Timothy. "They've got the yard all decorated and everything. But no one's there yet."

Before Frank could say, "Good one, kids!" Titus pulled out the scrap of balloon and showed it to him.

"Well, now," said Frank. "The way I see it, there's a difference between being nuts about your dog and being just plain nuts. And if you ask me, throwing a birthday party for your dog is a little on the nutty side."

"I agree!" said Titus. "It's just that I think Wags and Gubbio should have been invited, that's all."

Grandaunt Barbara had come in during this conversation.

"A birthday party for *Maggie*?" she asked. "That doesn't sound like something Sugar and Joe O'Hara would do."

"Maggie's owners," Titus explained to Timothy and Sarah-Jane.

"Sugar!" exclaimed Timothy. "Sugar? That's her name—Sugar?"

Barbara laughed. "A nickname. She's had it ever since she was a baby. *Everyone* calls her that. I'm not even sure I *know* her real name. Dear me, what is it? Margaret? Marian? Something like that. Anyway, even though she has a funny nickname, throwing a birthday party for her dog doesn't sound like something Sugar would do. Does it, Frank?"

"No, it doesn't," agreed her husband. "And even if Sugar and Joe did a nutty thing like that, you'd think they'd have the good manners to invite Wags and Gubbio."

"Sugar and Joe have lovely manners," said Barbara. "They're actually very rich, but they never make a big deal about it. On the outside, their house is quite ordinary-looking. But inside they have the most marvelous art collection! Timothy would love it!"

Before Timothy, who loved art, could reply, there was a knock at the door.

5

The T.C.D.C.

There on the doorstep stood the next-door neighbor, Mrs. Kimball, and her fluffy little white dog, Princess Snowball.

Mrs. Kimball was looking a little miffed. Princess Snowball was also looking a little miffed. But then Princess Snowball always looked a little miffed.

Titus had dog-sat for her a few times. And in his opinion, Princess Snowball was a spoiled brat. But he was too polite to say so to her owner. He knew what it was like to be nuts about your dog.

"I'm sorry to bother all of you," began Mrs. Kimball. "And I'm sure you'll think this is a most peculiar question. But did Wags happen to get an invitation to a birthday party?"

"No," replied Barbara. "As a matter of fact, we were just talking about that."

"There! You see!" cried Mrs. Kimball. "Princess Snowball didn't get one, either! Now, what do you think of that? I'm the last person in the world to make a big deal over something like this. But I don't mind telling you—I'm a little miffed."

"The whole party seems a little odd," said Granduncle Frank in his most calming way. "Not at all the kind of thing that Sugar and Joe would do. It's a mystery fit for the T.C.D.C."

6

Princess Snowball

*A*t first Titus was surprised that Princess Snowball and Sarah-Jane got along so well. But it made sense when he thought about it. Princess Snowball loved to be fussed over. And Sarah-Jane loved making a fuss.

The problem came when the cousins decided to leave the dogs in the yard and climb back up to the tree house. They wanted to get another bird's-eye view of Maggie's party.

Wags and Gubbio were fine with this. They were more than happy to stay on the ground and snooze in the sunshine.

Princess Snowball was not fine with this. As soon as Sarah-Jane set her down, she whined and howled and threw a little-doggy-hissy-fit.

"Ti!" wailed Sarah-Jane. "Make her stop!"

"Yeah, right," said Titus. "The only way she's going to stop whining is if she gets what she wants. And what she wants is for you to pick her up again."

Sarah-Jane picked her up, and Snowball stopped whining.

"This dog is a spoiled brat!" declared Sarah-Jane.

"Tell me about it," said Titus.

"So how am I supposed to get up to the tree house if I have to hold on to Princess Snowball?" asked Sarah-Jane indignantly.

Timothy said, "You can't put her in the basket and haul her up. She might jump out. And then there'd be trouble!"

"Let me try something," said Titus.

He ran into the house and came back a couple of minutes later with an old shoulder bag he had gotten from his grandaunt Barbara.

He explained, "Snowball is used to being carried around in a dog-snuggly. Maybe she'll think that's what this is."

He was right.

As soon as Titus hung the straps around Sarah-Jane's neck, Snowball wiggled into the bag and demanded to go for a ride.

It turned out that she was not the least bit afraid of heights. And she actually seemed pleased with the tree house that the nice children had built for her.

"I just hope she doesn't go nuts when she sees all those dogs at Maggie's party," muttered Sarah-Jane.

But that was the funny thing.

7

Bird's-Eye View

The cousins saw a few grown-ups coming and going. They saw balloons and streamers and a sign that said, *Happy Birthday, Maggie!* They even saw a pink-and-gray van parked in the driveway. It said *Carnival Catering* on the side.

But there were no dogs.

"That's funny," said Timothy. "Where are the dogs?"

"Maybe the party hasn't actually started yet," suggested Sarah-Jane. "Maybe those people are just helping to get it set up."

"Maybe," said Timothy. "But that still doesn't explain why they didn't bring their dogs."

Sarah-Jane said, "Do you suppose someone forgot to mail the invitations? Or do you suppose some of the invitations got lost in the mail?"

Titus shrugged. "It's possible, I suppose. But you'd think Sugar and Joe would have noticed the mistake by now. You'd think they'd be calling people, saying, 'Hey! Bring your dogs and come on over!'"

"Which ones are Sugar and Joe?" asked Sarah-Jane.

"They must be in the house," said Titus. "I don't see them there. I don't even see Maggie, and she's the guest of honor."

The cousins were quiet for a minute, thinking this over.

It must have gotten too quiet for Princess Snowball. She decided to stir things up a little.

She trotted over to the railing and barked down at Wags and Gubbio. You could have sworn she was saying, "Nyah, nyah, nyah. I'm up here with people, and you're not."

Wags didn't dignify that with an answer.

But Gubbio went nuts.

It's not that he wanted to be up in the tree house. He didn't. It's not that he minded his people being up there while he took a snooze.

He didn't. But no way was he going to let Little Princess What's-Her-Name move in on his territory and get fussed over by his people.

Titus groaned. "Oh, yes. This is working very well."

Timothy said, "I think these dogs need to go for a walk. And if we happen to walk by the party—? I wouldn't mind getting a closer look. Would you?"

"No," replied Titus. "I wouldn't."

8

Gate Crasher

"*F*orget it. I'm not carrying you. And that's that," Sarah-Jane said in a showdown with Princess Snowball. "If you want to go for a walk with us, you have to wear your leash. Period. And it won't do you any good to whine, young lady. You can whine till the cows come home, for all I care."

Princess Snowball looked at Sarah-Jane in surprise. So did Wags and Gubbio. Cows? What cows? They didn't have any cows.

Sarah-Jane took advantage of the moment to snap the leash on Snowball's collar.

Titus went to tell his parents where they were going. And then they were off.

It was the perfect disguise.

Three kids. Three dogs. Out for a stroll.

No one would guess they were three detectives out prowling around for clues.

"There's something odd about that catering van," Titus said.

The cousins walked past and glanced over at it—without being too obvious.

"What?" asked Timothy.

"I don't know," said Titus. "It just seems like something's missing."

"Why would you need a caterer for a dog-party anyway?" asked Sarah-Jane. "Dogs can't eat people food."

"No, but their owners can," said Timothy. "Maybe it's a party for the dogs' owners as much as for the dogs. Except—what dogs?"

The cousins walked to the end of the block. Then they circled back by way of the alley, where they would be able to see more.

They didn't really mean to do anything more than take a quick peek.

But Princess Snowball had other ideas. Maybe she was still miffed that Sarah-Jane had put her on the leash. Whatever the reason, she suddenly yanked free.

And crashed the party.

9

A Strange Conversation

The cousins had no choice but to follow Princess Snowball into the yard. They had hoped they could just grab her and get out of there. But Snowball was nowhere to be seen.

Instead they saw some dressed-up grown-ups putting something into the van.

And the grown-ups saw them.

One of the ladies came hurrying over. The cousins could tell at a glance that she was not pleased to see them.

"May I help you?" she asked in a voice that said that was the last thing in the world she wanted to do.

It was not easy to talk to someone who just wanted to get rid of you. But Titus knew he was responsible for Snowball, even though

Sarah-Jane had been holding the leash.

"Our dog ran in here," he said as he frantically looked around for her.

The lady looked around, too.

They all spotted Snowball at the same moment. She had somehow pulled a present off the table and was happily ripping it to shreds.

The lady gasped and lunged for her, but Titus got there first. He scooped up Snowball and started to pick up the present. It flashed through his mind that there was something odd . . . But before he could finish the thought, the lady grabbed the present out of his hands.

"I'm really sorry—" Titus began.

But the lady was in no mood to accept apologies. "Get that little dust bunny out of here!" she snapped.

Dust bunny?

Sure, Snowball was a spoiled brat, but there was no reason to call her names.

"She didn't mean any harm," he said. (This was probably not, strictly speaking, true.) "I don't think Maggie would mind—"

"*Maggie!*" exclaimed the woman. "How do you know Maggie?"

"She's a neighbor," said Titus.

"And I take it she likes children?" asked the woman. She sounded a little bit—a *tiny* bit—nicer.

"Maggie LOVES children!" declared Titus. "She's so gorgeous. And smart. Where is she? I want my cousins to meet her."

"She's not here right now," said the lady, smiling as though it hurt her lips to do it. "We're just getting the party ready. It's a surprise, you see. Do you think Maggie will be surprised?"

Titus looked at her, feeling very confused, to say the least. One minute this snotty lady was calling Snowball a dust bunny. And the next minute she was asking him in a phony, chirpy voice if he thought a poodle would be surprised.

It was a strange conversation where he understood all the words—but none of them made sense.

It wasn't the only strange thing.

There was the van . . .

And the present . . .

More than anything else, Titus knew he had to get out of there so he could think.

10

Carnival Catering

So Princess Snowball got her way after all. To keep her from running away again, Sarah-Jane picked her up and carried her.

Snowball didn't even get yelled at. Titus knew it wouldn't work. Whenever he tried telling her, "Bad dog!" Princess Snowball just looked around as if to say, "Really? Where?"

Besides, Titus had too much on his mind to yell at Snowball.

"Did you see the way that lady grabbed the present out of my hands?" he asked Timothy and Sarah-Jane.

"Yeah," said Timothy. "What did she think you were going to do? Steal it or something?"

"That's just it," said Titus. "There was nothing to steal."

"What do you mean?" asked Sarah-Jane.

"I mean, it was the lightest present I ever felt," said Titus. "It felt just like an empty box."

His cousins stared at him.

"Really?" said Timothy. "What kind of a dirty trick is that? Giving someone an empty box for a present."

"I suppose it could be something that didn't weigh very much at all," said Sarah-Jane. But she didn't sound as if she thought this was for certain.

"Could be," said Titus. "We wouldn't know unless we opened it up. And that lady got pretty upset when she saw what Snowball was doing."

"*Why* did she get so upset?" wondered Sarah-Jane. "Sure, no one likes to have a present messed up. But what would Maggie care? She would just rip it open herself."

They were quiet for a moment, thinking about this.

"And then there's the van," said Titus.

"What about it?" asked Timothy.

"Remember when I said I thought something was missing?" asked Titus. "Well, I figured out what it was. No address and no telephone number. Usually when you see business vans like that, they have the phone number painted nice and big. It's like free advertising when they drive around."

"Maybe they're in the phone book," Timothy suggested. "Let's check it out."

So they looked up Carnival Catering in the yellow pages. They couldn't find it. Then they checked the white pages. They couldn't find it.

Sometimes a phone book can be confusing, so Titus asked his grandaunt Barbara if they could call directory assistance.

"Well?" asked Timothy and Sarah-Jane as Titus hung up the phone.

"They have no listing for Carnival Catering," said Titus.

"Why would anyone paint a phony name on the side of a van?" said Timothy. "I have a really bad feeling about this."

"So do I," said Titus. "So do I."

Suddenly he also had a pretty good idea of what was going on over there.

But it wasn't enough.

He needed a plan.

Quickly he told his cousins what he was

thinking. And the three detective cousins came up with a plan.

But they realized it wasn't enough.

They needed a couple of grown-ups.

11

The Plan

*F*ortunately, it didn't take forever to tell the grown-ups what they wanted.

Granduncle Frank and Titus's father got in their cars and drove off.

Grandaunt Barbara wrapped a plate of cookies in aluminum foil and slapped a bow on top.

Then she took off one of her earrings and handed it to Sarah-Jane, who carefully put it in her pocket.

Titus's mother sat down by the phone and warned them all a dozen times to be careful.

Titus would have liked to have taken the dogs with them. But it was just too risky.

Grandaunt Barbara gave the cousins a head start.

They had trained themselves to move very, very quietly. They slipped into the yard next door to Sugar and Joe's and hid behind some bushes.

Sarah-Jane took the earring out of her pocket and rolled it into the party yard without anyone noticing.

A couple of minutes later, Grandaunt Barbara came sailing across the alley, carrying her plate of cookies. She walked right into the party.

"Helloooo!" she called. "My goodness!

I'm so glad I saw the decorations for the party. I almost forgot it was Maggie's birthday. And I *promised* her my special cookies. How could I forget when she knitted me that beautiful scarf? You must be Maggie's friends from the hospital board."

"Uh—that's right," said the snotty lady. "And you are?"

"Oh, just a dear friend from the neighborhood," said Grandaunt Barbara.

Suddenly she clapped a hand up to her ear. "Oh, don't tell me!" she cried. "Did I lose an earring? Oh, I hope not! Maggie's the one who talked me into buying them. Said they went with my eyes."

Grandaunt Barbara walked around the yard, studying the grass. When she came to where the cousins were hiding, she stooped down and picked up the earring Sarah-Jane had planted for her to find. "Here it is!" she called to the snotty lady. To the bushes she murmured, "You were right. I'll try to stall them. Run home and get your mom to call the police."

12

9–1–1

*I*t was almost impossible to make themselves slip out as quietly as they had come in. But the cousins managed to do it. One by one, they snuck out of their hiding place and into the alley.

It wasn't until they were safely out of sight behind a garage that they made a dash to the house.

Titus's mother called the police to report a burglary in progress.

Then she called some neighbors to come meet her in the alley where they would stand around chatting. Actually—standing guard.

The cousins knew it would be too noticeable if *they* hung around the alley. After all, they had made quite a commotion earlier. The party people were sure to wonder what they were doing back again.

But the cousins were far too restless to just sit there, twiddling their thumbs.

"I think these dogs need to go for a walk," said Timothy.

Wags looked at him as if to say, "What, again? What does a dog have to do to get a nap around here?"

But Gubbio and the "dust bunny" liked the idea. Snowball didn't even complain when Sarah-Jane snapped on her leash. But just to be on the safe side, Sarah-Jane and Titus traded dogs. Princess Snowball could be a pain, but Titus could handle her pretty well.

So the three cousins and the three dogs headed off.

It was hard, under the circumstances, to look like just three ordinary kids out for a walk with their dogs. But the cousins thought they pulled it off perfectly.

They didn't go up the alley, but went instead to the corner and turned up the next street. That way they were walking in front of Sugar and Joe's house again. Only this time they were walking on the opposite side of the street to be even less obvious than before.

The van was still parked at the side of the house.

Was it loaded up with the O'Hara's stolen art collection? Would the thieves try to drive off before the police got there?

It might be pretty hard—what with Titus's father and granduncle Frank sitting in their cars, casually blocking the driveway.

13

Something to Say

*T*itus hadn't quite realized how tense he was until he saw a couple of police cars pull up. Then he heaved a sigh of relief.

The police got out and talked to Titus's father and granduncle Frank for a moment. Then a couple of them guarded the front door while the other grown-ups went around back.

The cousins crossed the street and followed the grown-ups into the backyard.

At first the snotty lady tried to bluff her way out of it.

"Maggie O'Hara is a very dear friend of mine," she said to the police officers. "We serve on the hospital board together. Maggie does a great deal of charity work. And people like that so seldom think of themselves. I am simply setting up a little surprise party for her. Since when is that a crime?"

The lady flapped her hand in Grandaunt Barbara's direction. "Just ask this lady here. She, too, is a dear friend of Maggie's. Just ask her. She'll tell you."

"No," Grandaunt Barbara said. "I think my grandnephew has something to say to *you*."

The snotty lady looked right at Titus. "You again! Well, what is it? What do you have to tell me that's so important?"

"Maggie is a poodle," replied Titus.

14

Sugar, Joe, and Maggie

"*T*itus, how in the world did you keep a straight face when you said that?" exclaimed Sugar.

It was later in the day, and they were all gathered at Frank and Barbara's house. A neighbor had been able to track down the O'Haras. They had rushed right home to find that the thieves had *not* been able to get away with their art collection!

"Woof!" said Maggie. She laid her beautiful head in Titus's lap and gazed up at him as if to say, "My hero!"

"Woof!" said Gubbio. He managed to squeeze himself onto Titus's lap. He looked at Maggie as if to say, "*My* boy!"

"Actually," said Titus, patting both dogs,

"the fake party was a pretty clever idea.

"The crooks knew that neighbors around here keep an eye out for anything suspicious. They knew it would be pretty noticeable if a van pulled up and people were going in and out of the house.

"So they made the whole thing *less* noticeable by making it *more* noticeable. The crooks actually called attention to the house by hanging up balloons and streamers and even wrapping up some empty boxes. That way, when the neighbors saw people coming and going,

58

they would just think it had something to do with the party."

Timothy said, "It would have worked, too, if the crooks hadn't gotten carried away and put a name on the sign and on the balloons. They thought it would make the party more real-looking. But the problem was, they got the names mixed up."

Sarah-Jane said, "I know two different girls named Maggie. But I didn't know any *dogs* named Maggie—at least till now."

"Woof!" said Maggie.

Sarah-Jane laughed. "One of the girls—Maggie is her real name. It's not a nickname. But the other girl—Maggie *is* a nickname. Her *real* name is Margaret."

"Which is *my* real name," said Sugar. "But the only time I use it is on formal papers. Or with people I don't know well. People who know me call me Sugar. But no one *ever* calls me Maggie. In fact, when we picked that name for our poodle, I never even thought about it being short for Margaret. I just liked the name Maggie."

"Woof?" said Maggie. She was smart enough to know that people were talking about her. But she couldn't figure out why.

Joe said, "The crooks, it turns out, live not far from here. Neighbors, yes. But not good ones! They had heard that Margaret and Joe O'Hara had an art collection. They knew there was a dog. And they had heard the names Sugar, Joe, and Maggie. But they didn't know enough to know that Sugar was *not* the dog!"

Grandaunt Barbara laughed. "That's why they believed me when I said that Maggie helped me pick out earrings. They thought I was talking about a person. Anyone who knew the family well enough to throw a party would have known that Maggie was a dog. They would have said, 'Why, lady, you're just plain nuts. Maggie is a dog, and we're throwing a party for her.' "

"Which is also nuts," said Joe. "But may I make a suggestion?"

"Sure!" said Granduncle Frank. "Hold that thought—"

Because just then there was a knock on the door.

15

Maggie's Party

Grandaunt Barbara went to answer the door and came back with Mrs. Kimball. Mrs. Kimball had come to pick up Princess Snowball.

"Did my sweet little snookums have a nice afternoon with the children?" Mrs. Kimball asked the dust bunny.

Princess Snowball snuggled up against Sarah-Jane as if to say the two of them had had a perfectly delightful time together and that there could not be a more perfectly behaved dog.

"Isn't she adorable, Sarah-Jane?" exclaimed Mrs. Kimball.

Sarah-Jane opened her mouth, but no sound came out.

Mrs. Kimball didn't notice, because she

had turned to Sugar, Joe, and Maggie. "And how was the birthday party?" she asked.

Titus could tell that Mrs. Kimball was trying to sound polite. But she still looked a little miffed.

It took a while—quite a while—to explain that there had never been a birthday party.

Mrs. Kimball listened to it all with amazement and delight. "So what you're saying is that my precious little princess stopped a burglary?"

"Um—well, not exactly..." said Sarah-Jane.

"But think about it!" said Mrs. Kimball happily. "If Princess Snowball hadn't gone so bravely right into the party and started ripping open the presents—! Well, then! You wouldn't have gotten to talking to that *terrible* woman and realized the party was fake."

(Mrs. Kimball thought the woman was terrible. Not because she was a burglar. But because she had called Snowball a dust bunny.)

"Well—maybe when you put it that way," said Titus. He did not for one minute think Snowball was a good, brave little princess. But he didn't know what else to say.

"Woof, woof, woof!" said Snowball.

Titus could have sworn she was saying, "Nyah, nyah, nyah!"

"Joe!" said Granduncle Frank. "You never got to tell us your suggestion."

"Oh, right!" said Joe. "I was just going to say—that in all the excitement—no one took down the party decorations. So how about if you all come over to our house right now for pizza and dog biscuits? We can still have a party. Unless you think having a party for a dog is just plain nuts?"

"It's not the least bit nuts!" declared Timothy, who woke up Wags to tell him the good news. "It's neat-O!"

"So cool!" said Sarah-Jane, hugging both Snowball and Maggie.

"EX-cellent!" said Titus.

"Woof!" said Gubbio. And there was no doubt at all that he was saying, "That's my boy!"

The End

Series for Young Readers*
From Bethany House Publishers

★ ★ ★

THE ADVENTURES OF CALLIE ANN
by Shannon Mason Leppard

Readers will giggle their way through the true-to-life escapades of Callie Ann Davies and her many North Carolina friends.

★ ★ ★

BACKPACK MYSTERIES
by Mary Carpenter Reid

This excitement-filled mystery series follows the mishaps and adventures of Steff and Paulie Larson as they strive to help often-eccentric relatives crack their toughest cases.

★ ★ ★

THE CUL-DE-SAC KIDS
by Beverly Lewis

Each story in this lighthearted series features the hilarious antics and predicaments of nine endearing boys and girls who live on Blossom Hill Lane.

★ ★ ★

RUBY SLIPPERS SCHOOL
by Stacy Towle Morgan

Join the fun as home-schoolers Hope and Annie Brown visit fascinating countries and meet inspiring Christians from around the world!

★ ★ ★

THREE COUSINS DETECTIVE CLUB®
by Elspeth Campbell Murphy

Famous detective cousins Timothy, Titus, and Sarah-Jane learn compelling Scripture-based truths while finding—and solving—intriguing mysteries.

* (ages 7–10)